Clever Little Monkey

by Penny Dolan

Illustrated by Nicola Anderson

W

FRANKLIN WATTS

LONDON • SYDNEY

First published in 2015 by
Franklin Watts
338 Euston Road
London
NW1 3BH

Franklin Watts Australia
Level 17/207 Kent Street
Sydney
NSW 2000

A CIP catalogue record for this book is available
from the British Library.

ISBN 978 1 4451 3778 0 (hbk)
ISBN 978 1 4451 3780 3 (pbk)
ISBN 978 1 4451 3781 0 (library ebook)
ISBN 978 1 4451 3779 7 (ebook)

Series Editor: Jackie Hamley
Series Advisor: Catherine Glavina
Series Designer: Peter Scoulding

Printed in China

Franklin Watts is a division of
Hachette Children's Books,
an Hachette UK company.
www.hachette.co.uk

Monkey was hungry.

He saw bananas on the big trees.

He saw the river too.

How could Monkey get across?

The river was full
of crocodiles.

8

But Monkey was very clever.

10

"The longest crocodile
can eat me up,"
he said.

"Line up," Monkey told
the crocodiles.

"Let me see who is longest."

The crocodiles swam
into line.

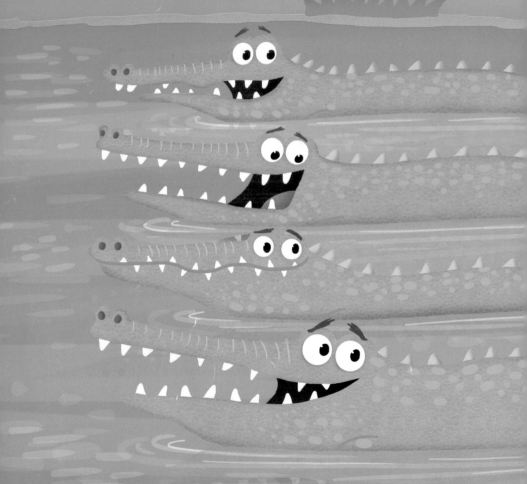

"Very good!" said
Monkey.

"Hmmm! Now let me see ..." he said.

Monkey ran fast as fast across their backs ...

... and up into the banana trees!

Puzzle Time!

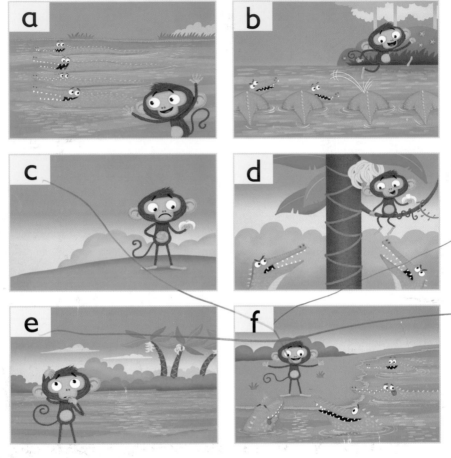

Put these pictures in the right order and tell the story!

cross

happy

fed up

delighted

Which words describe Monkey
and which describe the crocodiles
at the end of the story?

Turn over for answers!

Notes for adults

TADPOLES are structured to provide support for newly independent readers. The stories may also be used by adults for sharing with young children.

Starting to read alone can be daunting. **TADPOLES** help by providing visual support and repeating words and phrases. These books will both develop confidence and encourage reading and rereading for pleasure.

If you are reading this book with a child, here are a few suggestions:

1. Make reading fun! Choose a time to read when you and the child are relaxed and have time to share the story.
2. Talk about the story before you start reading. Look at the cover and the blurb. What might the story be about? Why might the child like it?
3. Encourage the child to employ a phonics first approach to tackling new words by sounding the words out.
4. Invite the child to retell the story, using the jumbled picture puzzle as a starting point. Extend vocabulary with the matching words to pictures puzzle.
5. Give praise! Remember that small mistakes need not always be corrected.

Answers

Here is the correct order:

1.c 2.e 3.f 4.a 5.b 6.d

Words to describe Monkey: delighted, happy

Words to describe the crocodiles: cross, fed up